"For Nathan, Will, and Karin. Thank you for inspiring me."
—Joanna Gray

Sandy Creek
NEW YORK

An Imprint of Sterling Publishing
1166 Avenue of The Americas
New York, NY, 10036

Text © 2013 by Top That! Publishing Plc
Illustrations © 2013 by Top That! Publishing Plc

This 2013 edition published by Sandy Creek.

Originally published by Top That! Publishing Plc
Creative Director — Simon Couchman
Editorial Director — Daniel Graham
Written by Joanna Gray
Illustrated by Dubravka Kolanovic

ISBN 978-1-4351-5254-0

Manufactured in China
Lot #:
4 6 8 10 9 7 5 3
5/15

The Little Raindrop

written by Joanna Gray

Illustrated by Dubravka Kolanovic

Sandy Creek
NEW YORK

One dark and stormy day, a little raindrop fell out of a cloud and flew faster and faster through the sky.

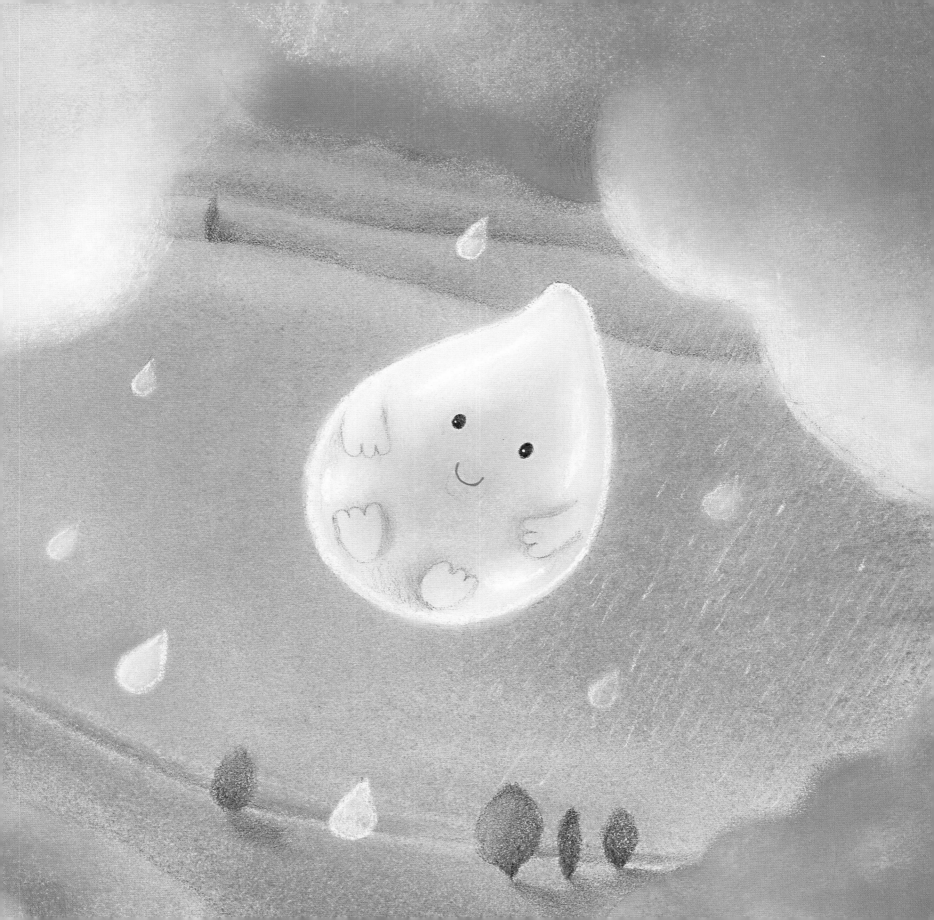

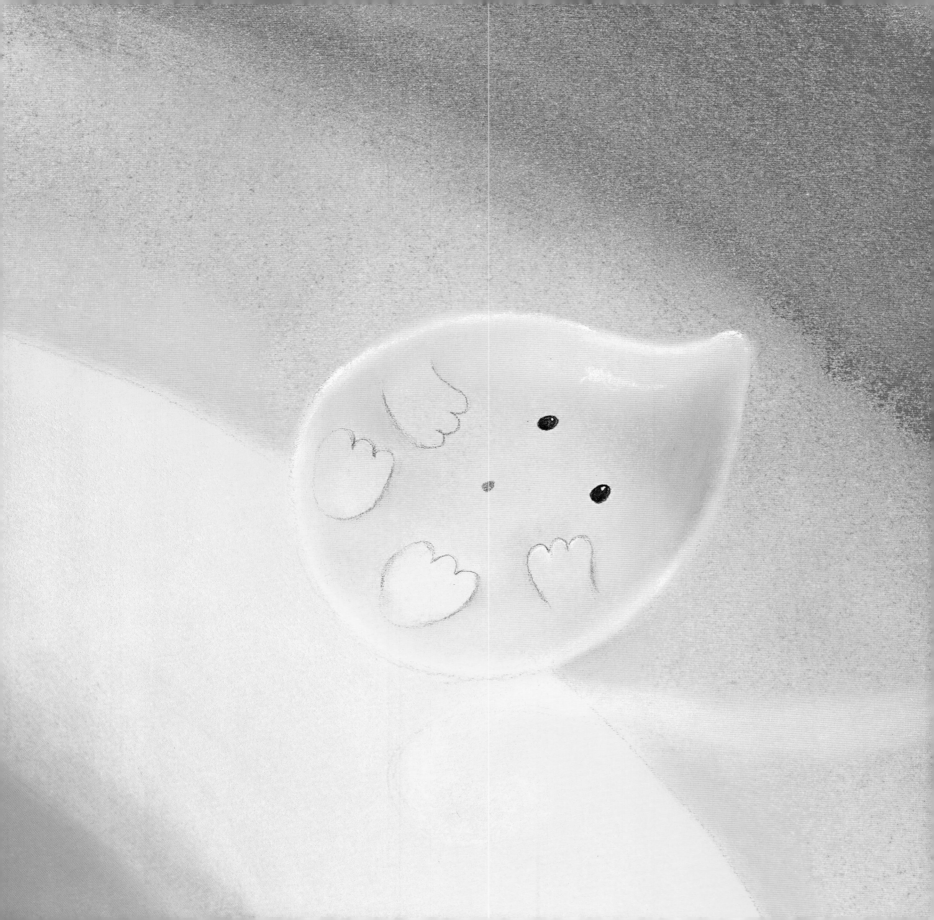

A gust of wind blew Little Raindrop sideways, and in a dazzling flash of red, orange, and yellow, he found himself inside a rainbow.

Enjoying the beautiful colors, Little Raindrop
fell through green, blue, indigo, and violet before
another gust of wind blew him out of the rainbow.

Splash! Little Raindrop landed in a shallow puddle on top of a large rock.

Splish! Splash! Splosh!
Lots of other raindrops fell all
around him, until the puddle
was overflowing.

Little Raindrop ran down
the side of the rock and
joined a stream.

In the stream, Little Raindrop drifted through woods and bounced over pebbles.

He played with small, shimmering fish
and watched them dart around
as deer and rabbits came to drink
at the water's edge.

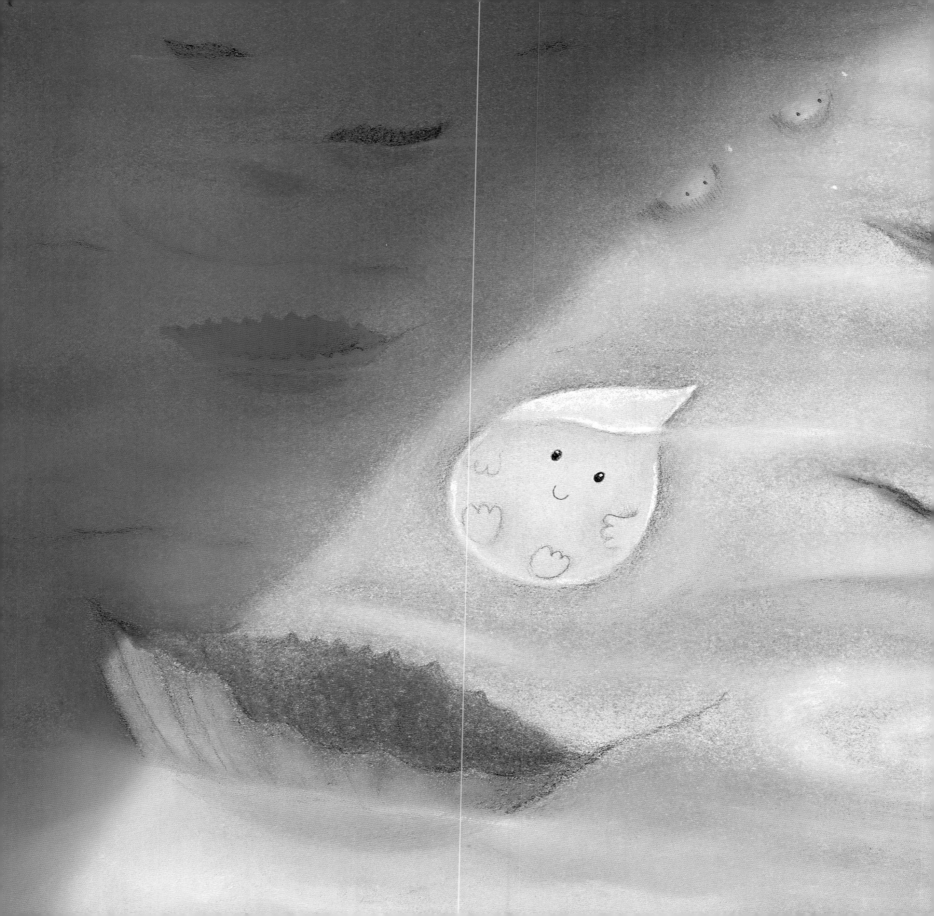

Sometimes, laughing children would race sticks in the water, and Little Raindrop would chase them under bridges, dodging the swirling grass and fluttering leaves.

After a while, the stream
joined a river, and Little
Raindrop floated along in
the strong current.

At times, the river was calm and peaceful,
and Little Raindrop watched diving kingfishers
and larger fish as they swam slowly by.

At other times, the river was noisy and rough. Little Raindrop raced along rapids and dived down waterfalls, carefully avoiding the jagged rocks at the bottom of the falls.

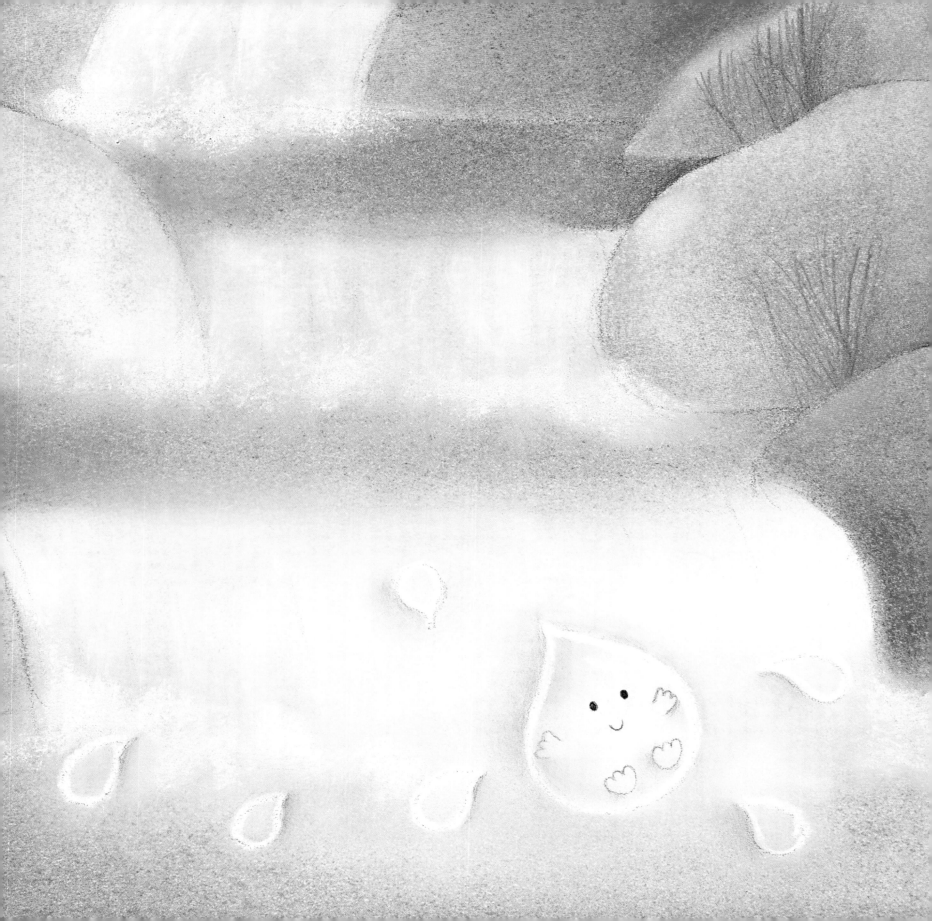

Eventually, the river reached
the sea, and Little Raindrop was
pulled far away from the shore.

He met friendly dolphins, who played and danced
in the sunlight, and listened as they whistled
and clicked their greetings to each other.

One day, the tide pulled Little Raindrop back to the beach. He surfed the waves and crashed onto the shore until finally he came to rest on the soft sand.

The sun shone down on the sand and Little
Raindrop got hotter and hotter, until the
warmth of the sun drew him up into the air.

It was cooler in the sky, and Little Raindrop
joined a cloud that was already
full of other raindrops.

Little Raindrop was ready to fall to Earth
and begin his journey once more.